Acting Edition

I0687892

Bike America

by Mike Lew

FOR PRODUCTION INQUIRIES

UNITED STATES AND CANADA
info@concordtheatricals.com
1-866-979-0447

UNITED KINGDOM AND EUROPE
licensing@concordtheatricals.co.uk
020-7054-7298

Each title is subject to availability from Concord Theatricals Corp.,
depending upon country of performance. Please be aware that *BIKE
AMERICA* may not be licensed by Concord Theatricals Corp. in your
territory. Professional and amateur producers should contact the
nearest Concord Theatricals Corp. office or licensing partner to verify
availability.

Winner of the 2012 Alliance/Kendeda National Graduate Playwriting Competition, *BIKE AMERICA* was originally produced by Alliance Theatre, Susan V. Booth, Artistic Director in Atlanta, GA on February 6, 2013. The performance was directed by Moritz von Stuelpnagel, with sets by Andrew Boyce, costumes by Melissa Schlachtmeyer, lighting by Matthew Richards, and sound by Kendall Simpson. The Production Stage Manager was R. Lamar Williams. The cast was as follows:

PENNY	Jessica DiGiovanni
RORIE/MARILYN/LAURALIE	Je Nie Fleming
TIM BILLY	Brandon Hirsch
TODD	Matt Nitchie
MAN WITH THE VAN/GENE/STUART/CARLO	Maurice Ralston
ANNABEL/PATTY/MOM	Marilyn Torres
RYAN	Tom White

BIKE AMERICA received its New York premiere by Ma-Yi Theater Company, Ralph B. Peña, Artistic Director, Jorge Z. Ortoll, Executive Director on October 1, 2013. The performance was directed by Moritz von Stuelpnagel, with sets by Andrew Boyce, costumes by Melissa Schlachtmeyer and Amy Pedigo-Otto, lighting by Matthew Richards, and sound by Jill BC Du Boff. The Production Stage Manager was David S. Cohen. The cast was as follows:

PENNY	Jessica DiGiovanni
RORIE/MARILYN/LAURALIE	Melanie Nicholls-King
TIM BILLY	Landon G. Woodson
TODD	Vandit Bhatt
MAN WITH THE VAN/GENE/STUART/CARLO	David Shih
ANNABEL/PATTY/MOM	Marilyn Torres
RYAN	Tom White

The play received workshops/readings from the Kennedy Center/ NNPN, the Lark Play Development Center, The Playwrights Foundation, The Juilliard School, Ma-Yi Writers Lab, and Ensemble Studio Theatre/ Youngblood.

CHARACTERS

The cast of 7 actors (3F, 4M) plays the following characters:

PENNY (F, 20s, any ethnicity) – our heroine

TODD (M, 20s, any ethnicity) – her clingy long–distance boyfriend

RYAN (M, 30s, any ethnicity)– a crunchy granola biking instructor

TIM BILLY (M, 20s, Black) – a cross-country bicyclist

ANNABEL (F, 30-40s, Asian or Hispanic) – a cross-country bicyclist/ Rorie's wife

PATTY – a Brooklyn artisanal cheese maker

MOM – Todd's mom, an Allentown she-bear

RORIE (F, 30s-40s, Black) – a cross-country bicyclist/Annabel's wife

MARILYN – a Connecticut homeowner

LAURALIE – a Kentucky bartender

MAN WITH THE VAN (M, 40s, any ethnicity) – a grizzled shamanistic porter

GENE – a Brooklyn artisanal cheese maker

STUART – an Ohio YMCA director

CARLO – an Arizona county clerk

SETTING

Time: 2014. Place: America.

AUTHOR'S NOTES

Set: You'll need some stationary bikes. Or you could also use half-bikes with the backs cut off and do bike puppetry. It'd be nice to have a big map upstage with the route marked on it and city markers that light up as they progress down the route. It'd also be nice to have video projections of the road. Ahhhh… it'd be nice…

Historical Note

Rorie has a line in the Arizona clerk's office (Scene 19) that references the number of marriage licenses they've attained thus far on the trip. During production, we've had to update that number as more and more states have legalized same-sex marriage. As of publication, the number of licenses they would have attained over this particular route totals seven (MA, RI, CT, NY, NJ, PA, NM). To contemporize the play, feel free to update the number if the legal landscape continues to change. Or in the event of national legalization, consider the play "frozen" in the year just beforehand.

1. Prelude

(Darkness. The sound of bicycle wheels clacking. Ding ding! A pool of light. **PENNY** *is center stage on a stationary bike, one foot on a pedal and one foot on the floor.)*

PENNY. Hi, I'm Penny. I'm a *fuckup*! I'm a lady adventurer. I'm, uh, I'm figuring out my shit.

(She starts to bike.) Right now I'm nearing the end of my cross-country bike trip, passing down Arizona's spine to the small of California's back. I've only lived in Boston, and I've never seen the Pacific, and I'd hoped that between these two points there could be some other life.

It's 2 AM, and the air's cold and dry, and I'm biking down the highway alone. Because – yknow – what can I say? I'm a fuckup.

In a few seconds some shithead truck driver will drift to sleep and his rig will drift to the shoulder and my bike will drift under his front right tire and that'll be the end of my ride.

But back up the road, up past Flagstaff and Austin and Memphis, up past the highways, and back up and back up and out, I'm at the gym in Boston training for the journey that'll cost me my life.

2. Boston, MA

(Lights shift abruptly and we're at the gym in Boston.
PENNY's *working out on the stationary bike.* **TODD**
enters.)

TODD. Penny I think we should talk.

PENNY. Not now Todd. I'm biking.

TODD. But this level of biking is nuts. I feel like I barely see
you. It's like all you do these days is go to classes, go to
the gym, go to classes, go to the gym. What about me
time? This gym stuff is tearing our fabric.

PENNY. Shut up.

TODD. No I will not shut up. This health kick has been
frickin' interminable! You've been at it for three or
four *days.*

PENNY. So what?

TODD. So it's making me *nuts.* What are you, training for a
triathlon, Penny?

PENNY. *(She stops.)* I signed up for the Bike America tour.
It's a three-month bike tour *for cancer.*

TODD. You WHAT? *(She goes.)* What do you mean you're
biking for cancer? What about us?

PENNY. What us?

TODD. Don't say "What us." We *have something.* I am your
boyfriend.

PENNY. No Todd. We talked about this.

TODD. Yeah but –

PENNY. I told you I'm not looking for a relationship.

TODD. Yeah but that was ages ago. I took your silent assent
for consent. I thought after grad school we'd maybe
move in together, maybe someday we'd walk down the
aisle…

PENNY. Whoa buddy we're not even boyfriend and
girlfriend.

TODD. Of course I'm your boyfriend. My toothbrush is on your sink. We visited my mom that one time. You're even wearing my shirt!

PENNY. Could we maybe not do this right now? I'm really not into labels.

TODD. Oh God, you're so emotionally distant. I have to have you!

PENNY. Come on Todd, I'm biking!

TODD. Oh and I love how you're biking for *cancer*. That way if I complain I'm an asshole. Take me with you.

PENNY. No.

TODD. Oh I see what this is. Is this because I'm physically weak?

PENNY. No, Todd.

TODD. Yes it is. You're acting out because I'm a noodle.

PENNY. It's not because you're a noodle –

TODD. So you *admit* I'm a noodle!

PENNY. I just need some time to sort some things out for myself.

TODD. Why? What do you think you'll find out in California?

PENNY. Fuckin' *fish tacos* Todd – the endpoint is so not the point. I'm 27 and I'm still in grad school. At 27 my mom had a kid and a house. My grandma had three kids and functional alcoholism.

TODD. I'm not following.

PENNY. Everyone gets to go on a journey like this to see what's out there and see what they're made of. This is my turn.

TODD. For *three months*? That's too long, Penny! When were you gonna tell me?

PENNY. Tomorrow?

TODD. Oh sure, "tomorrow," it's always "tomorrow." And when does this bike tour start?

PENNY. Tomorrow.

TODD. You WHAT?!

(Quick scene change. The gym falls away and **TODD** *falls back and other bikers come onstage on stationary bikes. They are biking America.)*

RYAN. That's good guys, keep up the pace. Look at that. We're almost outside of Boston.

PENNY. Fuck, fuck, fuck, fuck, fuck, fuck, fuck, fuck…

RYAN. This first couple days are the worst. You may have been training but nothing prepares you for biking 6 hours a day. Especially if the only training you've done is on a stationary bike at the gym.

(collective laugh)

PENNY. Fuck fuck fuck fuck fuck fuck fuck…

RYAN. That shit will NOT prepare you.

(The **MAN WITH THE VAN** *pulls up beside them.)*

Hey everybody it's the Man with the Van! Say hi.

ALL. Hi!

MAN WITH THE VAN. Hey how many miles to the gallon you get on those things?

(Beep beep!)

RYAN. The Man with the Van's going to drive ahead with our gear. Say goodbye to your stuff.

ALL. Bye!

MAN WITH THE VAN. Eat my exhaust, stinky bitches!

*(***MAN WITH THE VAN*** exits. ***PENNY*** wobbles, nearly falls, and recovers.)*

PENNY. Oh shit.

TIM BILLY. You doing all right?

PENNY. Yep!

TIM BILLY. You didn't train enough, did you? How long you been training?

PENNY. 4 days!

TIM BILLY. 4 days?! Shit, why didn't you train more?

PENNY. Shut up.

TIM BILLY. But you knew this was coming.

PENNY. No I didn't. I signed up for this trip 5 days ago.

TIM BILLY. Oh shit so you just decided to bike cross country on a whim. Like – what am I doing next Friday? Think I'll bike 4,000 miles.

PENNY. I'm a fuckup.

TIM BILLY. Of course not. Well kind of. So why'd you sign up so last minute?

PENNY. For cancer.

TIM BILLY. Well yeah for cancer but…

PENNY. But what?

TIM BILLY. I'm so sorry – do you know someone with cancer? Because…

PENNY. No. I don't know. FUCK so hurty – why.

RYAN. Bus coming up on your right. *(HONK HONK! WHOOOOOOSH!)* Hell yeah!

TIM BILLY. I'm Tim Billy by the way. Welcome to the ride!

PENNY. Tim Billy. The fuck kind of name is that?!

TIM BILLY. Uhm. The one my parents gave me?

PENNY. Sorry – the biking. So cranky. I'm Penny.

TIM BILLY. "Penny. Hello." See? This is how you greet somebody when they tell you their name. Not "What the fuck kind of name is that."

PENNY. Mine's better.

TIM BILLY. Ok and I'm going to push on ahead.

PENNY. This is – HRRR! – This is all part of the plan, Tim Billy. I believe that extreme physical duress can lead to an even greater epiphany.

TIM BILLY. *Epiphany*! Like what?

PENNY. Like my ass is on FIRE.

TIM BILLY. Hang in there. It gets easier.

PENNY. *(hopeful)* Yeah? Yeah you think my ass'll adjust to this seat?

TIM BILLY. Oh, the *bike seat*? No, you've got 4,000 miles of that. *(Lights down on him laughing.)*

PENNY. Thanks, Tim Billy! Thanks for reminding me we've got 4,000 miles of this shit!

(Lights up on **ANNABEL** *and* **RORIE**.*)*

ANNABEL. Left left left left left!

PENNY. Ahhhh!

ANNABEL. Did I startle you? Sorry.

PENNY. You should warn people.

RORIE. She did. She said, "Left."

PENNY. Ohhhh got it.

ANNABEL. I'm Annabel. On your left. This is my wife Rorie.

RORIE. Hey.

ANNABEL. You doin' ok, hon?

PENNY. I'm fine. I'm fucking invincible.

ANNABEL. We can call the Man with the Van.

PENNY. Don't need him.

ANNABEL. Well if you do, he's not just there to carry our stuff.

RORIE. Yeah he's also trolling for poop-outs.

ANNABEL. Rorie.

RORIE. What? I know how to spot me a poop-out.

PENNY. I'm not a poop-out.

RORIE. Shit, you poopin' out now.

PENNY. I *am* pooping out now.

ANNABEL. Hon, you can't be pooping out. We're only like 6 miles in.

PENNY. Fuck. Why did I do this? Why?

RORIE. Tell you why we did it…

ANNABEL. We're getting married!

PENNY. Congratulations.

ANNABEL. We're actually already married.

PENNY. Oh.

RORIE. In Massachusetts. But we're getting remarried in every state that we hit on this trip.

PENNY. Isn't that… illegal?

ANNABEL. Nope. As long as you're marrying the same person, you can get remarried in every state. Oh. But then there's the whole gay marriage thing. Which is, largely, illegal.

RORIE. That's why we're hitting city halls in each state. I want to make 'em say no to my face.

RYAN. Ok we're coming up on the bridge. Watch the trucks. Everyone call out the make and model of their bike.

RORIE. Bianchi Infinito Athena!

TIM BILLY. Cannondale Supersix 3 Ultegra!

ANNABEL. Raleigh Revenio 2.0!

RYAN. Raleigh Revenio 4.0, fuckaaaas!

ALL BUT PENNY. Oooooooh.

PENNY. *(pause)* Huffy I picked up at Target!

(They all turn and look back.)

Is that a good one?

3. Newport, RI

RYAN. *(sing-songy, signaling)* FU-UUU-LL STOOO-PPPP.

(Lights shift and **PENNY** *dismounts the bike.)*

PENNY. *(wobbling)* Ha na na na...

RYAN. Guys, how we feeling? *(General groans all around)*

PENNY. That wasn't so bad! I actually feel fucking great! Look at that sailboat!

RYAN. Guys. You just biked 70 miles. Give yourselves a round of applause. *(They clap. Eventually he kills it.)* That's good. Ok, we've got half an hour of free time but stay on the pier. Then it's off to our home stay. The Man with the Van should be waiting.

ANNABEL. Where's the home stay?

RYAN. College buddy's letting us crash in his 3-story Newport Victorian townhouse. Bastard. You've never seen this much wainscoting. Or crown molding. Or sconces. Are these real words I'm using? I feel like they aren't real words.

PENNY. Guys. We're in *Newport.* We're FREE!

TIM BILLY. Free from what?

PENNY. Let's go to an Irish shantybar and get shitfaced!

TIM BILLY. Penny go easy.

PENNY. Why? I feel *great.*

TIM BILLY. That's the endorphins talking. Your first night out, you're gonna feel great but you gotta protect yourself for tomorrow, see. Do your stretches. Take your potassium.

PENNY. That's great, Coach. Who wants a beer?

RORIE. *(Everyone but* **RORIE** *drifts off.)* I could be down...

PENNY. Hell yeah Rorie. Let's go to the Barking Crab and do oyster shooters. Let's do rum shots with the guys who wear popped collar Polos and boat shoes without any socks.

RORIE. I mean, I'm not down with all that – we're biking 60 miles tomorrow. *(She drifts off.)*

PENNY. FINE. I guess I'll just have to get shitfaced myself!

*(Lights down and up in a flash and **PENNY** is down on the floor, passed out, fondling a Polo shirt.)*

RYAN. Lights up! *(**PENNY** lets out a huge gasp.)* Good morning sunshine!

PENNY. Shushy shushy.

RYAN. We're on our way to Connecticut in 15 minutes exactly. You should be prepping your gear in 5.

PENNY. I can't move…

RYAN. *(quick and unaffected)* You're fine. *(exits)*

PENNY. I can't move myself. Cramps. *(shoots a leg out)* Leg spasm! I have a leg spasm. *(sits up)* Ow, hangover. *(shoots a leg out)* Leg spasm other leg! Ow, but again with the hangover.

RORIE. How late were you out last night?

PENNY. Rorie! Rorie, I can't move my legs. Uh oh, Rorie, whose Polo shirt is this? Whose shirt is this, Rorie, what's happening? Help!

RORIE. Ummmm… not my girlfriend. *(She exits.)*

PENNY. Regret. I'm feeling regret. *(points into the air)* Screw you for judging me sconce.

4. On the road through Connecticut

(By now, everyone but **PENNY** *is on their bikes.)*

RYAN. Penny, let's go!

PENNY. *(she gets up and hops on her bike)* Coming, I'm coming.

RYAN. Ok guys just follow my pace.

PENNY. *(even-paced)* Fuck fuck fuck fuck.

RYAN. And up the hill now...

PENNY. *(labored)* Fuck... Fuck... Fuck... Fuck... Fuck...

RYAN. Down the switchback.

PENNY. *(swerving)* Fuckety WAAAAAAAH. Fuck fuck fuckcakes WAAAAAH. Fuckcakes Johnson. EEEEEEE.

RYAN. Over the gravel bed.

PENNY. *(shaky)* fuuu-uh-uh-uh-uh-uh-uh...

RYAN. Aaaaand up the mountain.

(Everyone but **PENNY** *quickly ascends the mountain as* **PENNY** *keeps chugging. And chugging.)*

PENNY. Fuck...huh huh huh... Fuck... huh huh huh.... Ffuh... fuhhh... huh.... Huh... poopout.

ANNABEL. I see her! Penny, you made it! *(Everyone claps.)*

RORIE. Your first big uphill workout! You want an energy gel? Lemme get you an energy gel. *(exits)*

TIM BILLY. You need some water?

PENNY. I need... a *cyanide.*

RYAN. You're fine.

ANNABEL. Hey, do your uphill photo.

TIM BILLY. Yeah, lift your bike over your head.

PENNY. *(exhausted, exhausted by the notion)* WHAT?!?

ANNABEL. Just... lift your bike over your head. And we'll take your picture.

RYAN. Like this, see? HRRRRRR! *(He lifts his bike over his head and* **TIM BILLY** *takes a photo.)* YEAAAHHH LEVEL UP!!

ANNABEL. We all did ours while we were waiting.

PENNY. Um. Okay.

> *(She strains. She strains. She cannot lift the bike and ends up under it.)*

PENNY. Spot! Spot!

ANNABEL. Um. Maybe just stand by your bike lookin' diesel.

PENNY. *(sinking to her knees)* No stand. No bike. I quit the bike tour now leave me to die.

5. Darien, CT

(Twilight. The guys and **PENNY** *are standing on the porch of a tasteful Connecticut home.* **PENNY** *doesn't move her legs the whole time.)*

MARILYN. There you are.

RYAN. Aunt Marilyn! We MADE IT.

(He gives her a biiig sweaty hug, and she SHRIEKS!)

MARILYN. Oooh but you're *filthy*. Do you visit your mother like this?

RYAN. I mean she's not on the route but... probably.

MARILYN. Well the Man with the Van's been waiting for over 2 hours and let me just say he is not conversant in tea talk.

MAN WITH THE VAN. *(enters)* Yo stinky bitches. Your stuff's in the back. I'm hitting the bar. *(He exits.)*

RYAN. Thanks for having us, Aunt Marilyn.

TIM BILLY. Your home looks *amazing*.

MARILYN. Thanks, I take great pride in it. This is a historical district. The Connecticut Minutemen were barracked all down this road.

TIM BILLY. It's like a gingerbread house!

MARILYN. *(disapproving)* Mmm.

RYAN. Don't get used to this. Yesterday was swanky and so is today but the rest of the trip's gonna be hostels, church stays, YMCAs...

PENNY. Whoa whoa whoa church stays? Boo.

RYAN. We're on a budget. You know this.

MARILYN. OK!! Well there's clams that need steaming. Fresh pressed linguine. For dessert there's fresh strawberries. We went berry picking this morning.

PENNY. Heh heh. Berry picking. No way.

MARILYN. Will you be *showering* prior to dinner or shall I just hose you down?

RYAN. I'd *love* a shower Aunt Marilyn. Sweet! *(He runs inside.)*

MARILYN. Oh, great host, Ryan. *(to* **PENNY** *and* **TIM BILLY***)* Is this how the Millennial generation conducts themselves? I don't hear from him all year long and then he shows up covered in dirt.

TIM BILLY. Should we wait outside, or…?

MARILYN. Sure, why don't you wait here? You can take in the woods, enjoy that cool salt air from the Sound…

TIM BILLY. Not get our stank on your rugs…

MARILYN. There's that aspect too.

PENNY. I mean I'm fine waiting here. Cuz… I can't move my legs.

MARILYN. See? Everyone wins.

TIM BILLY. You seriously can't move your legs? *(He lifts one of her legs.)*

PENNY. Ow what the fuck?!

TIM BILLY. *(He laughs.)* I told you to do your stretches.

PENNY. You may or may not have.

TIM BILLY. You know we're biking another 60 miles tomorrow.

PENNY. It could happen.

TIM BILLY. And then 60 and 60 and 60 every day for pretty much 3 months straight?

PENNY. *Thank you* Tim Billy.

TIM BILLY. I'm just sayin' how you gonna bike 60 miles when your legs don't move?

PENNY. Ummmm… *Talent?*

TIM BILLY. Why punish yourself like this? Why are you on this trip really?

PENNY. Why are you?

TIM BILLY. Uhhhh – I wanted to meet sweaty bike chicks whose legs don't work.

PENNY. Really.

TIM BILLY. Yeah they can't run away and no one else wants 'em. What's your story?

PENNY. Look, I'm 3 years in to this stupidass grad program –

TIM BILLY. Oh really? What program?

PENNY. – Fucking bullshit studies with a minor in jackoff. It doesn't matter. What matters is I've never lived anywhere but at school or my parents' place and by next year I'll be living with my clingy long distance boyfriend all of five blocks from where I live now.

TIM BILLY. You've got a boyfriend?

PENNY. No. Not exactly. It's a distance relationship? I'm putting more distance between us each day.

TIM BILLY. Oh I get it. I get what this trip is. You're like a bikeaway bride.

PENNY. I'd like to think I'm going *to* somewhere, not away. I'm shopping.

TIM BILLY. For what?

PENNY. Shopping the country. For – I don't know. For where I should live and who I should be. Shopping for a place I can be myself.

TIM BILLY. But aren't you yourself?

PENNY. Sure but location informs on the self, don't you think? Like this place. Connecticut. Maybe I could play tennis and ship my kids off to boarding school and go digging for clams. That's what you do for clams, right, you dig?

TIM BILLY. The fuck do I know about clams? I'm from Austin.

PENNY. See exactly. What's it like living in Austin? Or Santa Barbara? Or any place really. What if there's some other life for me and I don't even know it? I guess that's why I'm here.

TIM BILLY. Plus that whole raising money for cancer thing.

PENNY. Sure, I mean that too. I mean: *Cancer.*

TIM BILLY. Uh-huh.

PENNY. It's just, like, I feel like my life is so bounded, you know? Like, "I'm on this path. This is your life. Don't stray from this path." But *why* this path? Did I even *choose* this path, and if not then what other paths are there? Like haven't you read *On the Road* or *Huck Finn* or *Travels with Charley* and imagined that you're the one in it?

TIM BILLY. *Huck Finn?!*

PENNY. Eeeeee. *Tom Sawyer* then. What if I got to be a lady Tom Sawyer? You never get to see a lady adventurer, right, so what if I got to be one. You think that sounds dumb, don't you? That sounds dumb. Never mind.

TIM BILLY. No, it's just… you also can't bike.

PENNY. So what? So what if it's only day two and I think I grew bone spurs? This is America! I want to be the hapless heroine in my own picaresque. I want to see where I fit in to the American landscape, try on each town, live like they live. I mean I've got to go *somewhere* right? Because if I keep on living in dead end Boston with that dead end grad school and my dead end life there, I'll seriously die.

(He laughs a little. The girls enter, both in veils.)

RORIE. We're married, we're married.

ANNABEL. Woooo!

TIM BILLY. Congratulations!

RORIE. Three states down, thirteen to go.

ANNABEL. Is this where we're staying? It's like a gingerbread house!

(RORIE and ANNABEL exit. TIM BILLY starts chuckling, then laughing.)

PENNY. What's so funny?

TIM BILLY. "I want to see where I fit in to the American landscape or surely I'll die." Like, for real? Why not just pick a place and don't *think* so hard!

PENNY. Because, like, "the unexamined life is not worth living."

TIM BILLY. Man, you really are getting a masters in bullshit studies.

PENNY. Fuck off.

TIM BILLY. You're like *Walt Whitman.*

PENNY. *Ok...*

TIM BILLY. You're like a *wheelie Walt Whitman.* No, you're like Tom Sawyer on a raft, only you don't know shit about rafting.

PENNY. Tim Billy come closer so I can smack you.

TIM BILLY. Pick one or the other. Either come here to smack me or I'll come over there and I'll uh...

PENNY. You'll what?

> (**TIM BILLY** *chuckles. A moment.* **PENNY**'s *phone rings.*)

TIM BILLY. You wanna get that?

PENNY. Nah.

> (**TODD** *appears elsewhere on stage, eating Little Debbie snack cakes.*)

TODD. C'mon c'mon. Pick up!

TIM BILLY. What if it's your boyfriend?

PENNY. He's fine. Plus it kind of hurts to move, so... Voicemail.

TODD. C'mon Penny where are you?

> (*Back in Boston,* **PENNY**'s *voicemail message kicks in.*)

PENNY. *(voiceover)* Hey this is Penny. I'm on a cross-country bike trip so don't expect a callback anytime soon. Oh, why did I say that? Nobody rob me.

TODD. It's Todd. Again. You know something? I do expect a callback soon because I am your boyfriend. So call me. *(pause)* You know, I hope you're happy getting a *sexy biker bod* on your little vacation because right now I'm on a staycation with Little Debbie. Great, I got icing on myself. YOU HAPPY?! *(meek)* Please call.

6. On the road to NYC

(Lights shift. Everyone but **ANNABEL** *is on their bikes.)*

RYAN. Guys, when we hit New York City I want no funny business.

RORIE. What do you mean by that?

RYAN. I mean what I said: no funny business. Where's Annabel?

RORIE. She got a call from her fam and pulled over to take it.

RYAN. See, this is exactly what I mean. You shouldn't have let her split off.

RORIE. I'm her wife not her mom. What's the big fuckin' deal?

RYAN. New York is dangerous, that's what's the big deal. You've gotta watch your gear at all times. You need kryptonite locks and steel chains going through both wheels and through the seat.

PENNY. I actually never bought a lock. Can we pick up a lock on the way?

RYAN. No. No, we're not stopping to shop in New York. If we stop in New York they'll rob us. Now the Man with the Van went ahead to set up a safe house in a neutral location.

RORIE. Look, no disrespect but I'm from Brooklyn and New York's not that hard. You're thinking of 80s New York.

RYAN. Oh am I? Last year I got my chain snapped, my tires bent, my reflectors knocked off, and my seat wet.

TIM BILLY. Seat wet?

RYAN. This was a brazen crime on a major intersection.

RORIE. Did you chain it to a street sign during alternate side parking? It probably got hit by a sweeper.

RYAN. Don't contradict me with weird Brooklyn talk. New York is dangerous.

(GENE and PATTY come pedaling by.)

GENE. Oh hey guys. Mind if we bike alongside you?

PATTY. Isn't it lovely this morning? We've been biking upstate all weekend.

GENE. Oh honey you're spilling the curds jar.

PATTY. Oops. Party foul! Ha ha haaa.

RYAN. Who are you? Where do you come from?

RORIE. *Ryan!*

PATTY. There's this amazing dairy upstate. The milk's fantastic but that isn't even the real draw. The real draw is the rennet, which is a certified cruelty-free rennet.

GENE. Those poor little calves.

PATTY. Look at how doughy and dense these curds are, and they've only been steeping an hour.

RYAN. Guys, I don't mean to alarm you but you're headed for Manhattan and by the looks of it those bike baskets don't have kryptonite locks.

RORIE. Don't mind him. Where you guys headed?

GENE. Through Manhattan and over the Williamsburg Bridge.

RORIE. Oh y'all are from Brooklyn?

PATTY. We started an artisanal cheese shop off Driggs and North 8th. Stop by there sometime.

RORIE. Fuck ya. I'm stopping by now. Do you have that one with the wax rind and the blue veins that's like *super* stinky? I fucking love that one.

TIM BILLY. I could go for that.

PENNY. Yeah!

RORIE. Oh and if we do stop in Brooklyn I'd love to drop in on my grandma.

TIM BILLY. *Awwwww.*

RYAN. No. No stopping, no cheese shops, no grandma.

RORIE. Ryan, what the hell?

RYAN. And you two don't fool me for a minute.

GENE. Don't *fool* you?

PENNY. Geez, Ryan, you're being a little bit harsh.

RYAN. No, I know. I know you New Yorkers. You know I know you New Yorkers. You think you're so unique...

TIM BILLY. Ryan what are you saying?

RYAN. I'm saying I don't trust you.

RORIE. Christ, Ryan, these are hipster artisanal cheese makers. Look at her thrift store jacket. Look at his old timey facial hair. These are not the mythical New York hoodlums you're so irrationally fixated on.

PATTY. No, dears, I'm afraid that we are.

(They jump off their bikes.)

GENE. Get off of the bike! Get off of the bike! Now now now now now!

RORIE/PENNY/RYAN. Ahhhh!

TIM BILLY. *(super-high pitched)* OHHHH GODDD!

PATTY. Toss everything in the bag! Wallets and clothes!

TIM BILLY. *(super-high pitched)* Oh God! Why do you need our clothes?

PATTY. Come on, come on - phones, jackets, anything lycra, anything bike gear, wallets...

RYAN. Not agaaaaaaain. I fucking *told you guys*.

(PENNY's phone rings.)

PATTY. What's that? Whose is that?

PENNY. Mine.

(TODD appears elsewhere onstage.)

TODD. Come on come on come on!

PATTY. What is that? An iphone? A droid?

PENNY. Motorola Razr.

PATTY. In chocolate?

PENNY. No, raspberry.

PATTY. Aw keep it.

PENNY. You sure? I mean you really can have it.

PENNY. *(voiceover)* Hey this is Penny. I'm on a cross-country bike trip so don't expect a callback anytime soon. Oh, why did I say that? Nobody rob me.

TODD. I just don't get… why aren't you…

*(**TODD** starts to cry a bit. Lights down on him.)*

GENE. Come on let's GO.

PATTY. Gotta run kids. Brooklyn Flea Market opens in an hour and these cheese curds won't poutine themselves.

GENE. Stay out of Williamsburg fuckos.

RORIE. With pleasure, ya shithead hipster artisanal bandits!

*(**GENE** and **PATTY** exit. Lights down on them.)*

RYAN. COCK GOBLINS!! *(pause)* I'm ok, I'm ok… SHIT ON MY FACE!! *(pause)* Is anyone hurt?

TIM BILLY. You OK?

PENNY. I'm fine. You kind of scream like a girl.

TIM BILLY. No I don't.

*(**ANNABEL** runs in, costume changed, gets on her bike, pedals hard, then hops off the bike.)*

RORIE. Annabel!

ANNABEL. Oh my god guys what happened?

PENNY. We just got robbed. They stole our clothes and Tim Billy's nuts.

TIM BILLY. I *don't* scream like a girl, ok?

RYAN. K, here's the deal. We're getting the fuck outta New York. Annabel, find the Man with the Van and see if he's still alive. Everyone else, I'm taking point so follow behind me and stay in a tight formation. Tim Billy you take the rear; don't dawdle. And Rorie?

RORIE. What?

RYAN. You'll forgive me if we don't stop at *grandma's.*

7. A phone conversation

MOM. Hello?

TODD. Gkkk. *(crying)* Gaaugghhh haaaa haaaaaughhhhh!

MOM. Todd?

TODD. *Mama.*

MOM. Todd, what's the matter?

TODD. She left me, Mama, she left.

MOM. Who did?

TODD. Penny!

MOM. Penny. Which one was Penny…. Ohhhh. Penny, right. I never liked that bitch.

TODD. Mom!

MOM. Penny told you she's a fuckup.

TODD. Mama my heart's bleeding out of me.

MOM. Son, when a girl says she's fucked up, it's not a challenge. It's a deterrent.

TODD. But…

MOM. No. When you hear, "I'm not into labels," that does not mean, "I need a savior." When you hear, "I'm not looking for a relationship," that does not mean, "I'm not looking for a relationship *but then came you.*"

TODD. But she's out there biking alone. I have to find her.

MOM. Oh, are you Audubon? Are you famed ornithologist John Audubon?

TODD. I'm not *Audubon,* Mom.

MOM. Then don't go looking for broken birds.

TODD. Mom, I have to go.

MOM. Really? You have to go, or you don't like what I'm saying?

TODD. I do. I have to go.

MOM. Don't go looking for broken birds, Todd.

TODD. I'm not.

MOM. You're lyin'. Every time you call me, it's all just cryin' and lyin'. I told you not to go to stupid-ass Boston. I told you to stay in Allentown and be a coal miner like your daddy but *oh no*, you had to go to Boston to become a professional crybaby.

TODD. I don't have time for this! I have to go find her!

MOM. Aht!

TODD. I mean... not find her. I just have to go Mom. I... bye. *(hangs up)*

MOM. Pussy.

    *(**TODD** cries.)*

8. On the road through New Jersey and Pennsylvania

RYAN. So. Anyone else want to second guess my directives?

RORIE, ANNABEL, TIM BILLY, PENNY. No…

RYAN. Are you sure? Nobody else has any bright ideas about where we can or can't stop? How about you Rorie?

RORIE. I fucking said no, boy, don't push it.

RYAN. Good. So when I say we're blowing through New Jersey no one would have a problem with that. Does anyone have a problem with that?

RORIE, ANNABEL, TIM BILLY, PENNY. No!

RYAN. Good. No eye contact and no conversation 'til we hit Pennsylvania. Not one fucking word. You got it?

(Various Jersey Passersby yell from offstage as the group trudges on.)

PASSERBY. Look at these fuckin' fucks on their bikes.

PASSERBY. Hey ya dumb fuck what ya think you're better than me cuz you're biking?

PASSERBY. Lookit these stupid fucks. What, you're on a bike so I'm s'posed to give a fucking fuck?

PASSERBY. Lookit these dumb fucks enjoying the pastime first popularized by French carriage-maker Pierre Michaux upon construction of his 1860s pedal-driven machine then known as a velocipede. What a buncha fucks.

BABY PASSERBY. You guys are doody-heads. You smell like doody. I'm a baby and I don't know any curse words but doody, YOU FUCK.

(Lights shift and they are still biking.)

ANNABEL. Oh shit. Is that… I think that it is.

PENNY. It's Pennsylvania!

(Everyone cheers.)

ANNABEL. Pennsylvania! We're saved!

TIM BILLY. Pennsyl-motha-fuckin-vania!

RORIE. Smell ya later Jersey!

PENNY. Puh-puh-puh-Pennsyl-va-zizzle. Whaaaaaat?

RYAN. Guys, guys! The enthusiasm is great, but we're going to be biking through Pennsylvania for a long fucking time.

TIM BILLY. Pennsyl-va-zizzle?

PENNY. Shut up. *(***TIM BILLY** *laughs. Lights shift as day turns to dusk.)* Oh hey. Five miles to Allentown. My ex-boyfriend grew up in Allentown.

RYAN. Yep, that's where we're staying tonight. Allentown.

ANNABEL. It's like *Paris*.

RYAN. I arranged an overnight with a Lutheran church.

PENNY. Aw shitstains. *Church stay.*

RYAN. It's fine. They're letting us use the basement. It'll be nice… nice basement.

PENNY. I kinda wanna sleep in a real bed. You think I could crash at his place?

TIM BILLY. Whose place?

PENNY. My ex-boyfriend's mom's place.

TIM BILLY. Now by ex-boyfriend do you mean… your boyfriend?

PENNY. He's not my boyfriend. He's my ex he just doesn't know it yet. It's a distance thing. We're in a distance but open relationship. Whatever, dude, I don't like labels. *(calls out)* Ryan! I'm going to pull off.

RYAN. No separating out from the group.

PENNY. Dude we're out of the Treacherous Tristate. You think you could maybe take it down a few *defcons*?

RYAN. It's not about safety, it's about group cohesion.

RORIE. I don't really have a problem with it.

ANNABEL. Yeah me neither.

TIM BILLY. Get that bike seat out of your ass.

RYAN. *(signaling as before)* FU-UUU-LL STOOO-PPPP. Fine. But in order to maintain cohesion I suggest bringing back snacks for the group, such as a number of Luna bars.

PENNY. Done.

RORIE. *(neutral)* You eat Luna bars. (**ANNABEL** *laughs.*)

RYAN. So?

RORIE. So those are for women!

RYAN. Nutrition is non-gender-specific.

RORIE. ...Do you take prenatal vitamins? (**ANNABEL** *laughs.* **RORIE** *and* **ANNABEL** *exit.*)

RYAN. Penny, this is very important. Be back at Saint Vincent's Lutheran on Saint Francis Street between 5th Street and 6th Street by 7AM so the five of us can get on the road by 8. *(exits)*

PENNY. Six Saint Street, Saint Seventh Street. Got it.

TIM BILLY. Hey, Penny?

PENNY. Yeah?

TIM BILLY. Take care of yourself.

PENNY. Softie.

9. Allentown, PA

(**PENNY** *dismounts and* **MOM** *enters.*)

MOM. Yeah?

PENNY. …Hi. Mrs. Morris, I'm Penny. I don't know if you…

MOM. I know who you are. I remember.

PENNY. I'm on a cross country bike trip and I was in town so I thought I'd stop by.

MOM. And why's that?

PENNY. To see you.

MOM. Yeah well ya saw me.

PENNY. Mrs. Morris can I stay the night maybe? My bike group's staying in a church basement – ew – so I thought I'd crash here with you.

MOM. Yeah that's not happening.

PENNY. Mrs. Morris. Did I do something wrong?

MOM. Why don't you ask Todd? Ask Todd whether he feels wronged.

PENNY. Todd doesn't *get* to feel wronged. #1: I told him I was leaving. #2: He calls all the time. And #3: this trip is for *cancer*. Shall we discuss this inside?

MOM. How about no.

PENNY. Duuuuude I just want to sleep in a real bed tonight. Don't the rules of hospitality say that you have to help out your son's friend… girl-*girl*friend?

MOM. Penny, you have been messing around with my boy's head.

PENNY. I'm being as straightforward as I can be about my particular *pro*cess.

MOM. No, no you're not. You're the kind of chick who says, "I just need to be alone right now," and then calls back at 2 in the morning sobbing, "Why am I so alone?"

PENNY. Uhhhhhh…. *(one octave higher) Uhhhhhhhhhhhhh…. (What's the play? What's the right response to that?)* Mrs. Morris, isn't this between me and Todd?

MOM. No, because you don't know what you want and you're dragging him through it!

PENNY. No, I *do* know what I want – he just won't hear it. I'm trying to do the right thing here but *dude.* He is NEEDY. He won't stop calling, won't stop *crying*, won't take a hint.

MOM. So what? You think Todd's daddy was a walk in the park? Every day I wanted to *kill him.* 'Til he died in that coal mine. But I stuck it out with him because that's what you do as a woman.

PENNY. But what if that's not the woman that I want to be? Why can't I be a lady Odysseus? Or why can't I be a dude? Dudes don't gotta call home every day. Dudes just go do what they want.

MOM. Look you. I don't care what you do do or don't do, but if you wanna stay here? You better get right with Todd and then get right with Jesus otherwise get the hell off my block. *(she exits)*

PENNY. *Fine.* (**PENNY** *dials her phone.*)

TODD. *(entering elsewhere onstage)* Hello? P-P-P-Penny?

PENNY. Yo, why's your mom such a dick? I'm in Allentown trying to crash and she's all like, "You can't stay here. You're tearing my baby apart." What the fuck! I'm just trying to stay out the church basement, know what I'm saying?

TODD. Penny just come home. Just come home and we can sort this all out.

PENNY. No, you call your mom and tell her you've been leading *yourself* on, not me. *(yelling)* I can see you in the window! Thanks for nothing, Mrs. Morris!

MOM. *(kind of muffled, maybe offstage or behind a window)* Get off my block! *(Bang bang!)*

PENNY. Dude, WHAT is your mom's PROBLEM? Why can't she be cool if we're cool?

TODD. Yeah but we're not cool. You ditched me.

PENNY. I didn't ditch you cuz we're not in a relationship.

TODD. If we're not in a relationship then why would my mom let you crash?

PENNY. Cuz we're *cool.*

TODD. Ah, but we're *not* cool. Penny you are not being very ladylike.

PENNY. You be the ladylike! You sit at home like Penelope, cuz I'm on my odyssey!

TODD. This whole bike trip thing's a charade.

PENNY. Don't call it a *charade.* Stop smothering me!

TODD. Dude! *You* called *me!*

PENNY. For fucking for *lodging purposes* Todd. But if you're not gonna help then forget it.

TODD. Penny wait! *(pause)* Penny I'm glad that you called me. Because it lets me know that you love me.

PENNY. *Todd.*

TODD. Ah-ah, let me finish, it lets me know that you do love me and you need me and for us to be cool I think you should drop the *charade* of this bike trip thing and come home.

PENNY. *(primal scream)* RRRRRRRR! *(She hangs up.)*

TODD. Hello?

*(***PENNY*** mounts the bike. She's rattled. Stupid Todd… Stupid Todd's Mom! Over the course of the below she gets more and more frantic. Think three hours of aimless biking compressed into 30 seconds.)*

Stupid Todd! Stupid Todd's Mom! Ok, St. Luke's on 16th St. No, wait, *this* is 16th St. *(she bikes)* Ah. St. Luke's. No, wait, this isn't St Luke's it's St. Paul's. *(bikes)* Ok another St. Paul's… Ok here we go 10th street - St. Peter's. St. Paul the Divine on 8th St. *(bikes)* Jesus, Saint Vincent's of 7th St, Our Lady of 6th Street. Saint – Fuck, what was it again? Ok here we go: St. Leonard's Avenue. Wait, that ain't right. Fucking Allentown! So many Lutheran churches! So many numbered streets…

(Later. **PENNY** *dismounts the bike.)*

TIM BILLY. *(whispering)* Penny? Are you ok?

PENNY. 'M *fine.*

TIM BILLY. What are you doing here? I thought you were visiting.... Hngghhh *(She kisses him forcibly.)*

PENNY. Shut up.

TIM BILLY. What time is it?

PENNY. Shut up I said. *(She kisses him more.)*

10. Pittsburgh, PA

(ANNABEL *and* RORIE *enter on their bikes.*)

ANNABEL. Huh...

RORIE. What's that hon?

ANNABEL. Pennsylvania's pretty big.

RORIE. I know, right? Pennsylvania you need to quit.

(PENNY *and* RYAN *enter.*)

PENNY. I could live here.

ANNABEL. Pittsburgh?

PENNY. Maybe.

RORIE. Ew, why?

ANNABEL. She's shopping for homes.

PENNY. For a place that feels like a home, where I can just be myself.

RORIE. Aren't you yourself right now?

PENNY. Well yeah but I can't stay on a bike trip forever.

RORIE. And this feels like home?

PENNY. Maybe it could. I've ruled out the Eastern seaboard.

ANNABEL. It's a little ugly.

RORIE. I'm *sayin'*.

PENNY. Why? You got steel girders criss-crossing the river. Honest folks in blue collar jobs. Industry. Bratwurst. The Loop. The Bears. Millennium Park.

RYAN. That's Chicago.

PENNY. Oh shit. That's not Pittsburgh?

RYAN. Chicago.

PENNY. All of it?

RYAN. The bratwurst's debatable, but everything past that for sure.

PENNY. Steel buildings then. And biker bars! Rusty steeples. Dude's dudes and... tough tits.

RYAN. What's a tough tits?

RORIE. Me!

ANNABEL. Yeah!

PENNY. Yeah and me too, if I lived in Pittsburgh.

(TIM BILLY *pulls up to* PENNY.)

TIM BILLY. Hey about last night.

PENNY. What about it?

TIM BILLY. I really wasn't asking for that.

PENNY. You kind of were asking.

TIM BILLY. I was asleep.

PENNY. Too bad. I'm a Pittsburgher tough tits.

TIM BILLY. You kind of raped me.

PENNY. Jesus. *I kissed you.* Don't just drop the word "rape."

TIM BILLY. There was forcible entry into my space.

PENNY. Grow up. You've been sniffing around since Boston.

TIM BILLY. You have a boyfriend.

PENNY. No I don't, I'm exploring. Like right now I'm exploring what it'd be like to be a Pittsburgher. Someone who works the steel mill *wasted* then spends all weekend hung over watching TV church.

TIM BILLY. I mean don't get it twisted. I like you. It's just I'm supposed to make the first move.

PENNY. Ohmigod Tim Billy get over it. IT WAS A KISS.

TIM BILLY. It just felt so violent.

PENNY. FINE, Tim Billy. I raped you.

TIM BILLY. Ok, maybe that is strong.

PENNY. Naw, fuckit. If you're going to be such a gentle flower then I'ma find me a new bitch.

TIM BILLY. What does that mean? Hey where are you going?!

(*Lights down on* TIM BILLY *and up on* RYAN.)

PENNY. Hey, Ryan?

RYAN. What's that?

PENNY. What's this I hear about the naked mile?

RYAN. (*laughing*) Huh huh. (*pause, coy*) The what?

PENNY. You heard me.

RYAN. I don't know what you're talking about. OK, I do know what you're talking about. Why do you want to know?

PENNY. The girls said something about it – said that you'd done it and I want to know what it is.

RYAN. I mean, it's kind of exactly what it sounds like.

PENNY. You ride a mile. Naked.

RYAN. *(shit eating grin)* That's right.

PENNY. And you've done it before?

RYAN. Several times, actually.

PENNY. I assume you do this at night.

RYAN. The first time. But then we did the naked mile pretty much all the time. It got *addictive.*

PENNY. I want to do the naked mile tonight.

RYAN. *You* want to do the naked mile.

PENNY. Yes, with no clothes on.

RYAN. So do it.

TIM BILLY. *(as though from afar)* What are you guys talking about?

PENNY. You're coming with me right?

RYAN. Sure, if you want.

PENNY. Ok so tonight.

RYAN. The naked mile. Tonight.

PENNY. Fuck yeah shitbird.

> *(Lights down. It is night. Total darkness on stage. Pedaling. Giggling. Giggling. Giggling. In the darkness we hear…)*

This can't be hygienic.

RYAN. This is like *so bad* for my sperm count.

> *(giggling)*

PENNY. I'm naked.

RYAN. *I'm* naked.

PENNY. I am riding a bicycle. NAKED.

RYAN. Fuck yeah. *Ow-oooooo! (wolf howl)*

PENNY. I'm FUCKING RIDING A BICYCLE NAKED! WOOOOOOO.

(The sound of wheels spinning but otherwise silence. Guess that's it, then. End of the scene. But no. A truck honks. They scream. The headlights flash and we see PENNY *and* RYAN *naked. Lights out again. Huge laughter.)*

We're doing this again at noon.

11. Boston, MA

(Back in Boston. **TODD** *is in ridiculous bike gear.)*

TODD. Penny. I feel a distance growing between us. You take off for months at a time. You don't frequently answer my frequent phone calls. And now you don't even respond when I text so I can only assume that you're entered a low coverage area. What am I supposed to do now? I think we both know what I'm supposed to do now: I'm coming to find you. That's right, I've got a Southwest flight and a foldable scooter and I'm going down South to find you. Since it's a Southwest flight they're charging 50 bucks for the scooter, every seat is a middle seat, and I'm inexplicably making a stop in Baltimore...twice. BUT I WILL FIND YOU.

12. Columbus, OH

(They are in the play room at a YMCA.)

STUART. It's really nice having you here. Gosh, biking across America. That'd be fun! Maybe.

RYAN. Thanks for hosting us Stuart.

ANNABEL. What is this place?

STUART. The K to 2 play room. Hope you don't mind.

RYAN. It's perfect.

PENNY. So Stuart. You're from Ohio. What is Ohio about?

STUART. Uhhhh... I'll try to stay out of your way. The gym closes at 10 and it's very quiet after.

PENNY. Does anyone use the gym? That equipment was looking brand new. You tell me, though, you're the expert on all things Ohio.

STUART. Uhhhh...

ANNABEL. What's sticky I'm stepping on? Is this candy or juice?

RORIE. *Annabel.*

ANNABEL. What?! Do they not have a mop?

*(**RYAN** clears his throat.)*

PENNY. No, really, Stu. What's it like being the swing state? Does being the decider make you feel powerful?

STUART. Powerful? I work at the YMCA.

RYAN. Penny where is this going?

PENNY. I want to know how it feels to be the decider.

STUART. Oh, I don't know...

PENNY. So – you're the decider... but you're totally indecisive. Huh. All my life I've felt like things were decided for me, but if I lived here then I'd be rewarded for indecision. You voted for Bush then Obama didn't you?

STUART. You're asking about the state of Ohio, or whether *I* personally...

PENNY. You.

STUART. Oh. Why yes I did.

RORIE. Wait, you did WHAT?

STUART. Well if you think about it the two weren't so different from a domestic policy standpoint.

RORIE. WHAT?!

PENNY. Oh my god Stu, you are my hero! Can I be the decider with you? Let's go to the bookstore and spend the whole night deciding whether or not we like books.

RYAN. Penny you're attacking our host.

PENNY. Oh no, oh no, I'm not. I'm so sorry, no. You don't feel attacked by me do you?

STUART. Honestly, yes. Well… I guess not, no. Look, if you're all set, I think I'll scoot out for some dinner?

RYAN. Yes, *please.*

ANNABEL. Um. Can we get a mop though?

PENNY. Wait Stu, don't leave. Where are you going?

STUART. Why I'm going home. Unless I want to eat out. But no, it's rather late, I think I'll go home.

PENNY. Take me with you, Stu. I want to study your ways.

STUART. Ummmmm… Ummmmmm….

RYAN. Sir, just go.

STUART. You're so peculiar. What a peculiar character. Can't decide if she's likeable… *(exits)*

ANNABEL. And… no mop.

RYAN. The hell was that?

ANNABEL. What? The floor's fucking sticky. These are facts.

RYAN. Do you know how HARD it is to find people who'll give us free space to crash?

TIM BILLY. A lot of guys voted for Bush then Obama. Why all the hate?

PENNY. What? I don't *hate* him. I want to *be* him. I want to move to Ohio and be the decider and never make a definitive decision ever again. Or do I? Yes, yes I do. No, what am I talking about – that's fucking crazy. Or maybe…

RYAN. Ok, we've got a long day tomorrow so everyone grab some floor.

ANNABEL. Do you think sleeping on a cubby is good? On the one hand less *sticky*, but on the other more *germy*...

RORIE. Annabel GO TO BED. Hey Ryan, after this do you think we could head west toward Iowa instead of south to Kentucky?

RYAN. No route changes Rorie.

RORIE. Come on! It's going to be hard as shit going to city halls in the South. We want another marriage certificate and you wouldn't even let us pop over to Vermont and New Hampshire.

RYAN. "Pop over?" No, we're not deviating from the route plan to suit your agenda.

RORIE. NO! Did you just say "your agenda?"

ANNABEL. Rorie, it's fine, go to bed.

RORIE. You go to bed! I already told you to go to bed.

ANNABEL. I'm not going to bed on this sticky-ass floor.

RORIE. Well nobody's moppin' it for ya, so go ta bed.

TIM BILLY. I'd like to go to bed...

PENNY. I'm not going to bed! Because I'm not even sleepy. Wait, am I? Yes, yes I am sleepy. No, I'm not sleepy. I don't know if I'm sleepy or not. I don't know what I am. I'm from Ohio.

13. Columbus, OH – hours later

(The YMCA. **PENNY** *quietly gets up and nudges* **RYAN**.*)*

PENNY. *Pssst.* Get up.

RYAN. What?!

PENNY. Shhh.

RYAN. I'm asleeping.

PENNY. You wanna have sex?

RYAN. *(fully awake)* Ok! *(They undress a bit.)* Wow, I didn't even know that you liked me.

PENNY. I don't.

RYAN. Cool.

PENNY. Let's break into the gym. They'll have air conditioning.

RYAN. You really don't like me? Not even a bit?

PENNY. Look, dude, let's not overthink it. This is not the start of a romance here, this is only a hookup. Now do you want this or not?

(He considers this. He breaks into a sprint for the door, dragging her after him. **PENNY** *laughs.* **TIM BILLY** *pops up.)*

TIM BILLY. Hey. Where you going?

PENNY. *(hiss-whisper)* Go to bed Tim Billy you had your chance.

14. Louisville, KY

(Thunderclap. A bar in Louisville. It's pouring outside.)

TIM BILLY. Why aren't you sitting with us?

PENNY. I'm good at the bar.

TIM BILLY. Penny am I wrong, or I thought we had a thing going.

PENNY. Maybe. But then you accused me of rape.

TIM BILLY. Come on! You wake me up at 3 in the morning and shove your tongue down my throat that's traumatizing. But that doesn't mean I don't want to get with you, girl.

PENNY. Dude, no. You're just gonna get all attached and I can't be having that at this juncture. Tim Billy, look at me: I'm a fuckup. Can't you see I'm a mess?

TIM BILLY. I mean yeah but it's *hot.*

PENNY. Tim Billy stop following me. Trust me. You're going to get hurt.

TIM BILLY. Oh God, you're so emotionally unavailable. I have to have you!

PENNY. Tim Billy, skedaddle.

TIM BILLY. But!

PENNY. Go on, now, git. *(He exits.)*

RYAN. *(enters, kisses her)* Hey here's a seat.

PENNY. *(momentarily ruffled, then recovers)* Hi.

RYAN. Hi!

LAURALIE. Well aren't you a sight. Never seen people bring a bicycle in here before.

PENNY. We're on a cross-country trip. Just waiting out the storm.

LAURALIE. Isn't that something. What refreshments can I provide you fine bicyclists?

PENNY. Can I get like a mint julep with mostly house bourbon but a splash of the good stuff to dull the cheapness, made really really strong but really sugary too so it's sweet going down but then you're like knocked off your ass?

LAURALIE. There's a name for that drink. It's called a surprise baby.

PENNY. OK, one of those!

LAURALIE. And for you sir?

RYAN. Gimme a double bourbon neat and a can of Coors.

LAURALIE. That'll be one surprise baby and one randy farmhand. *(exits)*

PENNY. You think I could live here? I could bet on the derby and see the Louisville Slugger Factory. I could see the Humana Festival. Whatever that is.

RYAN. How come you always pretend to live where we bike?

PENNY. I like it. I like imagining I can drop down in to some other life.

RYAN. What's wrong with this life?

PENNY. My life is. Claustrophobic. That's why I needed the road.

LAURALIE. Ok, here we go. Sip slowly lovebirds.

PENNY. Oh we're not lovebirds.

RYAN. Not yet that is.

PENNY. Fuck buddies.

LAURALIE. Sip slowly anyhow.

PENNY. Hey, so are you from Louisville originally?

LAURALIE. Mmm-hmm, all my life.

PENNY. Do you ever go to the derby and the Louisville slugger factory?

LAURALIE. No ma'am that's tourist crap.

PENNY. Oh. Oh ok so what's the *real* Louisville like?

LAURALIE. To be real with you it's real boring.

PENNY. No see, but I'm on this trip to figure out what makes a town tick. What life is like in each place we visit, what lifestyle suits me…

LAURALIE. Lord, you *tourists*. This town's not a Disney ride and I'm not your tour guide neither. I'm just a whiskey slinger, it's boring, this town's boring, you're boring, and I'm on a break. *(exits)*

PENNY. Well damn. Cross Louisville off the list.

RYAN. Don't worry. We'll be out of here as soon as this frickin' rain stops. Ugh. Rain days are the *worst* right?

PENNY. Eh.

RYAN. It's like – I'm a dragon slayer. That's what I do: I slay dragons. But you can't slay dragons in the rain.

PENNY. Hey tell me more about being a bike guy. What's that about?

RYAN. I don't know what that means. At this point you're pretty much a bike guy.

PENNY. No, but you're like a real bike guy. Could I be a bike guy? I bet you make your own bike out of bike parts. You're probably one of those guys who eats a good breakfast. What's the deal with oatmeal?

RYAN. I don't do any of that. Before I started taking these trips I was high all the time.

PENNY. Oh…

RYAN. Does that disappoint you?

PENNY. You just seemed so solid, you know? Like "I am a bike guy. That's what I am."

RYAN. But I am a bike guy!

PENNY. It's not you. I'm just a little… untethered. No town feels right for me and we don't even stay long enough to know what a town really is. I thought if I found the right place that everything would start to make *sense*. You think that sounds dumb, don't you? That sounds dumb. Never mind.

RYAN. No, hey, don't censor yourself, *let it out*.

PENNY. Fuck I might as well have stayed in Ohio. At least then I wouldn't have to decide what to do with my life. But no, no I do have to make a decision at some point. It's just… I thought life would unfold on these roads like a great American novel. I thought there'd be big answers hidden in the landscapes, dancing along the side of the highway.

RYAN. Nope. All there is is a string of towns from Boston to Santa Barbara. Some of it's pretty but most of it's flat.

PENNY. Ughhh, what am I doing?

RYAN. Ohhhh. Now I get it.

PENNY. Get what?

RYAN. "Ughh what am I doing" is the rallying cry of the 20-something. What are you, 26? 27?

PENNY. Yeah.

RYAN. Yeah, yeah, ok, I got what you need, check it out! Your 20s suck. That just a fact. Nobody wants to admit it's a fact because everyone wants to pretend that their 20s are some kind of magical summer but the truth is once you hit 30 it gets muuuuch better. You want a big revelation but you can't force it like they do in the books because get this Penny: you're not looking for a place, you're looking for time.

PENNY. *No.* What am I supposed to do, sit still several years 'til I feel better? Don't condescend to me because of my age. You're like 4 years older than *me.*

RYAN. Okay… *(defeated, he is about to go, when…)* You know, if you're feeling untethered? Talk to the Man with the Van. He sort of saved me, sort of turned me around. Back home he's an EMT? This one January I was high as a kite roaming Boston Commons half naked and I fell asleep in the snow. He found me and says to me – I'll never forget this – he says, "The fuck are you *doing here,* stupid? Why don't you get your *shit together* and put some clothes on!" That summer we were doing the naked mile.

PENNY. The Man with the Van. Turned your life around.

RYAN. Yep.

PENNY. But all he ever says is "I'm going to a bar," or "I'm going to a tit bar," or "look at those tits."

RYAN. Seriously talk to the Man with the Van. He's seen everything. Before he was an EMT, he was a carpenter. Before that he was a roadie for Creed. Trust me, if you're setting up concerts for Creed every night you're going to learn about coping with disappointment. And before that, the Navy. Here, he can tell you.

MAN WITH THE VAN. Lauralie, darling, another round of the bourbon.

LAURALIE. Get it yourself!

MAN WITH THE VAN. Heh heh. Look at her tits.

RYAN. Hey, Penny's feeling a little bit down. She could use a dollop of wisdom.

MAN WITH THE VAN. That so little Penny? Here's a small tidbit I learned in the Navy. When you're abroad and in port you'll naturally want to stock up on roosters, but the key here is to go for the happy and plump ones and not for the mean and stringy. That way, by the time you hit International Waters and can finally start up a cockfight, the plump happy roosters will have turned mean and stringy, whereas the mean stringy ones will have died.

PENNY. That's…. words to live by. That's… just what I needed, man. Thanks. *(glares at* **RYAN***)*

15. Memphis, TN

PENNY. You know something? Maybe you're right. Maybe this trip isn't about finding some perfect place. Maybe it is time. Time on my own. This trip is the first time I've ever experienced anything resembling real freedom.

RYAN. Look so... what are we?

PENNY. *What?* Ryan: No. What'd I just say?

RYAN. I'm not sure. I'm real nervous.

PENNY. We agreed that this was a hookup.

RYAN. No I know we did, *then.*

PENNY. No there's no *then.* That's what we agreed.

RYAN. It's just... we seem like we're having a really good time. I like you. I like biking with you, even though your form's pretty sloppy. Why can't it be more?

PENNY. Because I'm feeling simultaneously trapped and displaced as I desperately struggle to figure out my own shit. Is that a sufficient explanation for you?

RYAN. Ok so why don't you let me fix you? Hey, I've been there before. Let me fix you real good like a broken down bike.

PENNY. *(200% disgust) Jesus.*

RYAN. I just... I think we have a connection.

PENNY. Connection? There's only five of us on this trip, and the only thing keeping us sane between hundred mile stretches of flat nothing is talking with each other to pass the miserable time. *(She speeds on ahead.)*

RYAN. Oh God, you're so nihilistic. I have to have you!

(Lights up on the girls.)

ANNABEL. You doing ok hon? You seem like you're a little bit blue.

PENNY. I *am* blue.

ANNABEL. Well look on the bright side. It's Memphis. This is the perfect place for having the blues. Yeah, I could tell that you're blue though. Why are you blue?

RORIE. Is it because you fucked all the guys on this trip?

ANNABEL. Rorie!

RORIE. What, am I wrong? You fucked all the guys on this trip, then you mindfucked them, and now they want nothing to do with you. Tell me I'm wrong.

PENNY. Yes Rorie you are wrong. I'm blue because I'm unsettled, not because of a boy problem. Also I didn't fuck Tim Billy we only made out. Also I didn't mindfuck anyone.

RORIE. Then why are they avoiding your ass? Why are you biking with us and not them? What, we're best friends now?

ANNABEL. It's not her fault if these dudes come to her. Last time I checked it takes *two* to fuck. Two or two plus.

PENNY. Thank you Annabel.

ANNABEL. Solidarity.

PENNY. Seriously, all I want to do is bike and mind my own business. And maybe have a quickie no cuddles. I'm just trying to live like a dude and do how the dudes do but all I get back is the weepies. Tom Sawyer never had to put up with this shit.

RORIE. Tom Sawyer wasn't a slut.

PENNY. *All men* are sluts.

ANNABEL. I know *that's* right. I get it Penny. It's not your fault. They want to claim you but you're your own woman out on the road.

PENNY. Yeah. Yeah maybe.

ANNABEL. But you're not a dude.

PENNY. I'm not?

ANNABEL. No hon, you're a Memphis tough tits. And you can't be chained by these dumb boys and their constant demands. Cuz you're right. How come a guy gets to hook up with whoever he wants but a girl can't?

PENNY. Yeah, preach it feminist Jesus!

ANNABEL. *(to RORIE)* Apologize for calling her slut. That was very hurtful.

RORIE. Oh brother. I'm sorry, whore.

PENNY. It's fine betch.

ANNABEL. See, that's nice. Female solidarity.

PENNY. Maaaaan, fuck *all* these clingy bastards. Paint me a fence motherfuckas *I'm out.*

ANNABEL. Hey look up there. It's the Mississippi River crossing. Come on!

RORIE. No, we're going the other way down to Jackson, Mississippi.

ANNABEL. Aw, come on, it's right there. How many times in our lives will we ever get to cross the Mississippi River? Come on Penny.

RORIE. No, this way!

ANNABEL. *(to PENNY)* Go go go go go go go!

(At this point maybe we bring on three real working bikes. RORIE stops at one side of the stage. ANNABEL and PENNY bike to the opposite side.)

ANNABEL. Hey Penny check this out. *(yells)* Rorie!

RORIE. Come back over the bridge you daft twats.

ANNABEL. *(yells)* RORIE!

RORIE. What??!!

ANNABEL. We're the toughest tits West of the Mississippi!

RORIE. Yeah? Well I'm the toughest tits East of the Mississippi.

(ANNABEL laughs. ANNABEL bikes back to RORIE.)

ANNABEL. No, I'm the toughest tits East of the Mississippi.

RORIE. *(biking to PENNY)* Well I'm the toughest tits West of the Mississippi.

PENNY. I'm the second toughest tits West of the Mississippi!

(They burst into speed on their bikes, pedaling all over the bridge.)

ANNABEL. I'm the toughest tits crossing the Mississippi!

PENNY. I'm the toughest tits on top of the Mississippi!

RORIE. I'm the baddest troll of the bridge!

ANNABEL. Woooooo!

PENNY. I'm the toughest tits slightly southwest and above the Mississippi! *(She lifts her bike.)* HRRRRR! Take my picture! Take it! WRAAAAAAH!

(RYAN and TIM BILLY enter.)

RYAN. The fuck are you doing on that bridge? We're supposed to be going to Jackson.

RORIE. Fuck you guys!

ANNABEL. Suck on my balls!

PENNY. The Mississippi River's my bitch!

(TODD enters.)

TODD. Penny?

PENNY. Holy shit.

TODD. Penny I found you.

PENNY. Todd? Holy shit.

TIM BILLY. Who's Todd?

ANNABEL. Holy shit, Todd, are you riding a scooter?

(Lights down.)

16. Jackson, MS

(Johnny Cash's "Jackson" plays. Lights up on **PENNY** *alone on the bike, kind of like at the beginning of the play. She's pedaling for her life. Ding ding!)*

PENNY. Just make it to Jackson, just make it to Jackson, just make it to Jackson. *(Ding ding!)* Just make it to Jackson, just make it to Jackson, just make it to Jackson... *(Ding ding!)*

(Lights up on **RYAN.** *)*

RYAN. Penny I think this could be a relationship here. *(Bike horn – honk honk!)*

PENNY. Not now! Just make it to Jackson, just make it to Jackson... *(Ding ding!)*

RYAN. Come on Penny, I just want to talk. *(Honk honk!)*

(Lights up on **TODD** *on the scooter.)*

TODD. Penny? Penny can we talk about this? *(A cell phone sound – Ring ring!)*

(Lights up on **TIM BILLY.** *)*

TIM BILLY. Penny where did you go? *(A truck sound – Beep beep!)*

PENNY. Just make it to Jackson, just make it to Jackson... *(Ding ding!)*

TODD. Penny I need to know where we stand. *(Ring ring!)*

RYAN. Where *you* stand? Penny what is he talking about? *(Honk honk!)*

TODD. Just talk to me Penny. *(Ring ring!)*

TIM BILLY. I have to have you! *(Beep beep!)*

RYAN. Penny watch out. *(The sound of a truck passing – like the end of the play.)*

TIM BILLY. Just talk to me Penny. *(Beep beep!)*

TODD. Come on Penny. *(Ring!)*

RYAN. Penny, Penny, Penny? *(Honk!)*

ALL THE GUYS. Penny!

(A cacophony of sounds: bikes and phones and trucks.)

PENNY. Oh my god shut up! Shut up and leave me alone!

(A dead stop. The mood turns suddenly sober.)

ANNABEL. Whoa. You guys. Look. It's New Orleans.

TODD. Whoa. New Orleans.

RORIE. That's deep.

RYAN. Heavy, man, heavy.

RORIE. So deep. So emotional.

ANNABEL. Because Mardi Gras. But also. Katrina.

TIM BILLY. I have so many emotions about New Orleans. So much to say.

RYAN. I really just want to stay in New Orleans for a good long while and discuss all the things that I'm feeling.

(Blackout and all of a sudden we are in Austin.)

ANNABEL. Oh my god Texas is *so pretty.*

RORIE. I love Texas! Austin is fuckin' amazing!

ANNABEL. Weeeeeeeee!

17. Austin, TX

(Lights down on the girls and up on **PENNY** *and* **TIM BILLY**.)*

PENNY. Hey.

TIM BILLY. Hey.

PENNY. So how's it feel being home?

TIM BILLY. It's fine.

PENNY. Are you going to see your parents?

TIM BILLY. My dad's stationed in Okinawa and my mom died of cancer.

PENNY. Oh. Oh man. I'm so sorry.

TIM BILLY. Why? I love Okinawa.

PENNY. Why didn't you say something about your mom?

TIM BILLY. Why else would I be on a bike tour for cancer?

PENNY. I mean we all have our reasons. Marriage equality, self discovery, love of being inside of a van. Look, if you ever want to talk about it...

TIM BILLY. I really don't.

PENNY. Sure, ok... Well the Greenbelt is awesome. If I grew up here I would've ridden here all the time.

TIM BILLY. Yep.

PENNY. I could live here. Ride the Greenbelt. Go to blues clubs. Go fishing in the Colorado River.

TIM BILLY. Don't... don't do that. This is my home. Don't do that thing where you try on a town as you pass it by.

PENNY. I'm just saying I like it.

TIM BILLY. You know nothing about Austin.

PENNY. But I could. If I lived here.

TIM BILLY. But you don't. You're a tourist.

PENNY. Tim Billy why are you being like this? I'm trying to do the right thing.

TIM BILLY. You never even gave me a chance. We had a thing going – we had a flirtation – and then you move to the next guy like it means nothing, just like you move to the next town like it means nothing.

PENNY. But it *does* mean nothing. I kissed you and then you freaked out. I'm not, like, the girl of your dreams am I? Because take a hard look. Look at how sweaty and gross and gangly I am on this bike. I haven't shaved my legs in three weeks.

TIM BILLY. None of that matters.

PENNY. Seriously? Because this isn't just stubble this is like brambles.

TIM BILLY. You know maybe instead of passing everything up you ought to set down for a minute. See where you're at. Maybe if you weren't so scared you'd find something.

PENNY. Maybe. Anyway, boring. Look I can't be your girlfriend, I'm sorry.

(Lights down on TIM BILLY *and up on* RYAN.*)*

PENNY. Hey.

RYAN. Hey.

PENNY. So I'm sorry I can't be your girlfriend.

RYAN. Don't worry about it. We're cool.

PENNY. Seriously?

RYAN. I'm over it. Big time.

PENNY. Well if that's the case then I'd love to sleep with you.

RYAN. Nah I'm good. Like I said, I am over it.

PENNY. Really?

RYAN. In New Orleans the women wouldn't stop flashing me, and I didn't even have any beads. In New Orleans these triplets from Shanghai found me in the French Quarter and carried me – physically carried me – to their sorority house at Tulane whereupon we commenced a ménage a quattro.

PENNY. That's... good, I guess. You're exploring too.

RYAN. Oh I'm so exploring I'm Vasco de Gama. I'm charging the bend. See ya.

PENNY. Oh... ok.

*(Lights down on **RYAN** and up on **TODD**.)*

TODD. Oh, hey Penny! I caught up to you, good. I think I'm finally getting the hang of this long distance scootering. Ow! Rock. Rock in my shoe.

PENNY. Todd, you've followed me halfway through Texas. I think that you've made your point.

TODD. What point? This isn't a point. This is love. I'll be the Pallas Athena to your Odysseus. The Sancho Panza to your Quixote. The –

PENNY. Todd, go home.

TODD. But I want to experience what you're experiencing.

PENNY. This was supposed to be *my* experience. Mine.

TODD. But you clearly were seeking something and I want to know what you're seeking. I want to know so that I can provide it. Maybe it's like *The Wizard of Oz* and you're really just looking for home.

PENNY. I'm pretty sure that's not it.

TODD. Penny I come seek you out and there's all of these other guys but I don't even let that bother me cuz I know they're not me and deep down I know that I'm the guy that was made for you cuz I love you. I love you Penny. Doesn't that mean something?

PENNY. *(She stops dead.)* Ok, look. Yes, it means something. But you're going to have to stop saying that. When you say that, I don't know how to process it, and the fact that I don't know how to process it makes me feel guilty, and ultimately guilt is not the emotion you're trying to evoke in me when you say that, so stop it.

TODD. But I do love you.

PENNY. Yeah, and I loved you too, maybe. But only as – particle Penny. But I'm not a particle anymore, I'm a wave, so stop trying to pin me down to one spot.

TODD. What the hell does that mean?!

PENNY. I'm not sure because I dropped out of physics. But here's what I do know, Todd: I'm a wave. There's multiple Pennies out there living in each of these cities and I'm not yet ready to choose one, not nearly. I'm trying to find myself, and it's not gonna happen with you around telling me how I should be.

TODD. But... but. *I* found you. I came all this way and I *found you* Penny. What more do you need?

PENNY. For me to find me.

TODD. I just. I just thought that this effort would mean something. I thought that you'd see me... and and be moved by me... and and and maybe you'd weep, and I'd hold you, and and the clouds'd part and the frogs would be like, "Good job Todd!" And then maybe...

PENNY. And then maybe I'd still be as lost as I ever was. Look dummy I can't be your girlfriend. I'm sorry. Now will you please go home Todd? I'm begging.

TODD. But. But can't we just see if taking this trip *together* we...

PENNY. No, Todd, I'm tired of slowing my pace to 4 miles an hour so you can keep up on a Razor scooter. *(She speeds up.)*

TODD. It's really hard going over dirt trails with this. Stop, stop! I can't go that fast! Fine, I'll learn to ride a bike!

PENNY. It's not about the *bike*, Todd.

18. El Paso, TX

(Lights down on **TODD** *and up on the girls.)*

RORIE. Uh-oh, it's Dora the Explorer! What are we exploring today?

PENNY. Mind if I ride with you? Just thought I'd give the boys space.

ANNABEL. Boys. Who needs 'em.

PENNY. Hey, what is that, Mexico?

RORIE. Right across the river.

(They stop.)

PENNY. Damn. That's crazy.

ANNABEL. Yikes.

PENNY. We could go there. We could *escape.*

RORIE. Um. That's Juarez.

PENNY. So?

RORIE. So that's not Spring Break Mexico, that's drug wars Mexico. That's kidnap you and boil you in a vat of acid Mexico.

ANNABEL. No one escapes to Juarez, you ass clown, everyone runs away from it.

PENNY. Is it really that bad?

RORIE. It's a place where they *boil you in a vat of acid.*

ANNABEL. Why do you want to escape to Mexico anyhow? You'd be in complete isolation from everybody you know on this earth.

PENNY. Maybe it'd be good to get a fresh start.

RORIE. As what? A coke mule?

PENNY. Shit man. I know I have every advantage in this world but I just need a sense of direction before I can make a decision. Right now I've got no direction but west and that's only going to last 'til we hit the ocean.

RORIE. So go south then, you hate your life so much. Nobody's stopping you. Man, fuck this.

(She starts pedaling. Lights down on **RORIE.***)*

ANNABEL. What's up her ass?

PENNY. She hates me. Everyone else does.

ANNABEL. No. Come on. No. That's just her way. Sure, she's tough on the outside, but break through the outside and inside you'll find a real bitch. *(apologetic)* I better catch up. She'll accuse me of taking sides.

PENNY. Sure go ahead. **(ANNABEL** *is about to go, but...)* It's not like she says. For the record. I don't hate my life. It's just that this trip'll be over soon, and... And what if we hit the Pacific and nothing changes?

ANNABEL. Penny, are you really looking for a place or are you looking for people? Look, I've been there. Before I had Rorie I was... *Hoooo*, life is rudderless sometimes, I get it. But what I found, personally? And people told me this, and I ran away from this, and you may not wanna hear this, but the only way out of feeling rudderless? Is with love.

PENNY. *Lovieeeeeees. Luvy DUUUVIES.*

ANNABEL. What the... what is that?

PENNY. I gotta tell you: unvarnished sentimentality makes me SUPER-antsy.

ANNABEL. Penny, you do need love. You're on this self-discovery trip and I get it, hon. But for my part? I didn't know who I was until I found her.

PENNY. Are you seriously suggesting I need to seek definition by finding a man?

ANNABEL. I didn't say a man – I said love.

PENNY. Come on Annabel. If anything I should be cutting them off. Maybe if I reach the Pacific free from any obligations I'll finally get some clarity.

ANNABEL. But you can't just sever your connections.

PENNY. Why not? I'm not even sure I believe in love.

ANNABEL. *(She sizes* **PENNY** *up.)* Ok you know something Penny? I have something to show you. When we get to New Mexico, come to our wedding. Ooh, no. Arizona. Come to our wedding in Arizona.

PENNY. What, the city hall thing?

ANNABEL. Yes, the city hall thing. I'd like you to be a witness.

PENNY. You want me to... Really?

19. Flagstaff, AZ

CARLO. Next?

RORIE. What's happening, Jack?

CARLO. It's Carlo.

RORIE. We're here to get married and-uh-here is our form uh-thank-you.

CARLO. *(looks at the form)* Aw jeez.

RORIE. Aw jeez what?

CARLO. Come on, don't… don't come in here and give me a hard time.

ANNABEL. Who's giving you a hard time? This is a joyous occasion.

CARLO. Ladies, I'm just a county clerk.

ANNABEL. So get clerking with the "dearly beloved" already.

CARLO. I can't do that because I'm just a clerk. I am not a judge, I am not the governor, I am not a congressman…

RORIE. And you never will be, with that attitude.

ANNABEL. Yeah Carlo, think positive.

CARLO. No, you know something? This is bullshit. I know what you're doing, I don't respect it, and I can't change Arizona state law to fit your agenda.

RORIE. NO! Our "agenda." Our *agenda* of wanting our equal American rights. Our *agenda* of committing to someone we love and wanting the legal protections to support that commitment. Oh, I'm so sorry our *agenda* is spoiling your perfect Arizona evening. You know what – forget the marriage license. We want a handgun.

CARLO. Dammit! This is a place of a business. This is not a place for your politicking and grandstanding. Now you can take it up with me or you can take it up with the cops.

RORIE. Oh I would LOVE to take it up with the cops. You grab the sheriff and we'll grab the news cameras.

CARLO. LADIES. It's four-forty five and I'm really not into having my world rocked. I just wanna heat up a Hot Pocket and ride out the day.

RORIE. Oh no no no…

ANNABEL. Ok, tag out.

RORIE. CARLO!

ANNABEL. Tag out I said! *(They tag out.* **ANNABEL** *approaches, all sweetness.)* Look Carlo. All we want is to get married like everyone else. We love each other, we're committed…

RORIE. Plus we're already married in 7 other states so suck on that.

ANNABEL. All we ask is that you submit the paperwork. You can't change the law but what you can do is take responsibility for your own actions. Maybe we won't get a license. Maybe the paperwork stops with your supervisor and it never gets out the door. But *you* can do this one act of civil disobedience and push the paperwork one step forward.

CARLO. No. I can't. I can't and I also don't want to. Now do you want the handgun? Because that I can do.

ANNABEL. *(to* **RORIE***)* Go.

RORIE. You pencil pushing pencil dick. Grow some balls!

CARLO. Here, if it's any consolation I can offer you this. *(He hands her a flyer.)*

RORIE. "Free tequila tasting for you and your friends at the Flagstaff Distillery." What is this?

CARLO. I won it in a raffle. I was going to take my friends at the county clerk's office but – really – I want you to have it.

RORIE. Are you fucking nuts? I ask for my basic human rights and you hand me a *coupon?*

CARLO. No, you're the ones putting this on me, so this coupon is all I can do. Now take your little veils outside.

RORIE. Or what?

CARLO. Or nothing! We close in ten minutes and I make $7.50 an hour so my sole responsibility to you is to sit here and ride out the clock. If you make a ruckus I will lock myself in the break room. If you make a mess then the janitor will come clean it up. But Lord help me I will not call the cops if it helps your cause and I will not take your papers if you think that it gives you some kind of personal victory. I am done with your little charade.

RORIE. Oh, so our lives are a charade to you, huh?

CARLO. That's not what I said.

ANNABEL. Oh bullshit that's not what you said.

RORIE. You remember this moment. You remember that you had the chance to make the right choice – act with conviction here – and you blew it. That's not us putting it on you, that's who you are. *(CARLO is reduced to cowed, downward facing silence.)* That's right little man, turtle up. *(to ANNABEL)* You ready?

ANNABEL. *(PENNY starts to exit, but…)* Hey hey. Are you seeing this? Are you seeing what real love looks like? What a true *commitment* looks like?

PENNY. I mean there's a lot going on here…

ANNABEL. No. Fuck your flighty flighty bullshit and pay attention here. You wanna run away from all your connections? Deny love, pretend you're above it? Well don't. Love gives us purpose. These people hate us because of our love so for you who gets offered it freely? You be grateful for every last soul who loves you because love is something you fight for. Every time. Got it?

(RORIE and ANNABEL exit leaving PENNY there dazed. CARLO's watch alarm goes off and we beep-beep transition to…)

20. Flagstaff, AZ

(The distillery. Everyone's drunk but **PENNY** *and the* **MAN WITH THE VAN.** **PENNY**'s *curled up into herself, contemplative and disturbed.)*

TIM BILLY. I mean yo man this tequila factory's *awesome*.

RYAN. We were sposed to stay in a hostel. Not a tequiza sistillery.

RORIE. You said it's hard to find us a splace to crash in so I found us-sa-splace.

ANNABEL. Yes you did baby.

RORIE. I had the, um. Coupon. But who knew they'd let us stay for the night?

ANNABEL. Arizona's so friendly!

RYAN. Sup now girl you ready ta get in on this drinkin'? *(points to a dumb hat he has on)* Hey. I've got hat.

PENNY. I'm good.

ANNABEL. Come onnnnn! Join ya *family*.

TODD. Yeah Penny come down a stool and pull up a shot! Wait, that's not right…

RORIE. Todd, you're adorable.

ANNABEL. Honey we're gonna adopt ya.

TODD. Okay!

PENNY. I'll pass. On that drink. I just… need some lucidity right now if that's all right with you.

TIM BILLY. Shit thas not what she was sayin' in *Newport*.

RORIE. Righhht? Oh shit! What's this shirt? Omigawww NO – What's this *shirt? (laughter)*

RYAN. How 'bout you big man? You ready ta drink?

MAN WITH THE VAN. Naw man I'll have what she's having. Lucidity sounds pretty good.

   *(**MAN WITH THE VAN** and **PENNY** lock eyes.)*

RYAN. Aw you guys are fulla shit.

TODD. Yo man can I just say? *(lingers)*

RORIE. Say what little Todd?

TODD. Sorry I blacked out a little. Yo can I just say that I am in LOVE. With this BIKE.

(All but **PENNY** *cheer.)*

TIM BILLY. That thing is SMOKIN'. Lookit him – he won't even park it outside!

TODD. Brand new Kona Cadabra with Shimano hardware and hydroformed tubing.

TIM BILLY. What does that even mean?

TODD. I don't know! *(they laugh)*

RYAN. Buddy you kicked *ass* on that riverbed run.

TODD. You guys, I'm a *biker* now!

(Group laugh. **PENNY** *gets up, tries to leave quietly.)*

ANNABEL. Hon where ya goin?

PENNY. I just need some air.

TODD. Oh I see what's happening. Are you *jell-looousss* of my smokin' hot *biiiike*?

PENNY. No the bike's *great* Todd, it's great. It's great you're a biker. It's great that you've found your *people.*

TODD. What does that mean?

ANNABEL. Come on. Why you bein' like that?

PENNY. Look, fun as this is, I can't *sit here* and drink myself into oblivion. Not after what you said at your wedding.

ANNABEL. Naw, come on, Penny, forget that a minute. I know seeing two badass women exploded your brains, but can't you let it go for one night?

PENNY. No, actually, I can't. I can't because wherever we go I don't feel right, nothing feels right, and whiny and onerous as that may be at least I'm doing you the courtesy of taking my crisis outside.

TODD. I called it. Jealous of my bike.

RYAN. Kablamo!

PENNY. You guys, seriously. I am in crisis, it's real, and I'm sick of being mocked for it and I'm sick of your pat advice. *(to* **TODD***)* You want me to come home to you? Well I can't. *(to* **TIM BILLY***)* You want me to pick a place and don't think so hard? Well it matters to me, ok? It matters. *(to* **RYAN***)* You want me to wait til I'm 30 but what if I wait that long and I still feel as empty as I do on this trip?

ANNABEL. Penny.

PENNY. *(to* **ANNABEL***)* And you. You want me to love and embrace connection? Don't you know I'd do *anything* to feel love like you do? But right now I don't feel connected to any of you, I'm sorry, I don't. And I know that's my fault and I know that that's terrible and I probably don't even deserve love but I just want the space to figure this out on my own is that *really* too much to ask?

MAN WITH THE VAN. Looks like someone's having a Millennial moment.

PENNY. Arrrgghhh. *(She exits.)*

RYAN. The fuck was *that?*

TIM BILLY. Seriously. *Millennials.*

RORIE. Aren't you a Millennial?

TIM BILLY. Oh yeah. Shit now I gotta take a selfie and Instagram it with the sad filter.

TODD. Hashtag freakooouuut.

RYAN. Hey hey she doesn't like being condescended to because of her age. It says so right there on her Facebook wall.

ANNABEL. Guys. She's hurting.

RORIE. And that's our problem? *Please.*

ANNABEL. It's *everyone's* problem when we're still being formed.

RORIE. Hey I got a problem. I need a drink.

(The **MAN WITH THE VAN** *slips out. During this time,* **PENNY** *has been bicycling alone in the Arizona desert like her life depends on it. Lights down on the group and up on her…)*

21. The Arizona Desert

(PENNY *is still bicycling.*)

PENNY. Just make it to… somewhere. Just make it to somewhere, just make it to somewhere, just make it to somewhere, just make it, just make it, just make it, just make it…

(*Eventually her tire blows out.*)

PENNY. Frickin' DAMMMIT. (*she gets down to inspect the tire*) Awwwwww. Come on! Unbelievable!

(*She is at a loss. Stillness and crickets and desert. She takes in this pathetic situation. Just standing there, alone. Then the* MAN WITH THE VAN *appears.*)

MAN WITH THE VAN. Blowout, huh?

PENNY. *What the* – you were following me?

MAN WITH THE VAN. I'm the Man with the Van. Following you is my job.

PENNY. You're fired. Now beat it.

MAN WITH THE VAN. You weren't leaving us, were you? Just out for a stroll?

PENNY. My… itinerary is open.

MAN WITH THE VAN. Better find you some shelter before it gets cold. You feel that chill coming? Desert nights, man. Desert nights are the best. You forget. At least I do, stuck in that van. But out here, now? With the crickets and coyotes and stars. No smog, no atmosphere. Lonely nights. Nights like this there's not another soul around for a hundred miles.

PENNY. Are you going to murder and bury me?

MAN WITH THE VAN. Jesus, how can you say that?!

PENNY. It just seemed like a murderous preamble. Like, hey Penny, "there's not another soul around here for miles." CRACK. (*She mimes cracking somebody's neck.*) So if you're gonna do it then do it because I've got shit to take care of.

MAN WITH THE VAN. What a little shit. I'm trying to convey the wonderment of nature and you accuse me of murder?

PENNY. Well I don't know *what* your motive is, seeing as how you just stand there all smug while I'm stranded.

MAN WITH THE VAN. Yes, and how is it we got ourselves stranded, exactly?

PENNY. I don't know *Socrates*. What can I say. I'm a fuckup.

MAN WITH THE VAN. Yeah. You are.

PENNY. Hey!

MAN WITH THE VAN. That was a pretty epic rant back there. That was like Pol Pot ranting, only without the empathy.

PENNY. This is an emotional time.

MAN WITH THE VAN. No, the Led Zeppelin reunion was an emotional time. Your thing was more like a car wreck. *(He gets down to fix the tire.)*

PENNY. So what? They're being condescending as fuck. I'm on a huge search here and all I get back is stupid advice that fits them and not me.

MAN WITH THE VAN. Yeah I don't know. This isn't a genuine search.

PENNY. Of course it is. I feel *homeless*. Like it's either stay in this little box of a life or have no life at all. And I'm searching for a place where I can be in my skin and I'm searching for people who will let me be who I am, and yeah, I'm searching for genuine love, and… *(The* MAN *makes a fart noise.)* And did you just fart noise at me?

MAN WITH THE VAN. I don't know, did it sound like *(He makes a fart noise.)* Wow. You are more self-absorbed than a Sham-Wow. The fuck are you *doing here*, stupid?

PENNY. I need to *move*, okay? I *wish* I could settle down like they want but I have to lead an examined life. And that's not just a childish notion. That's an inherently American notion that goes back for hundreds of years, so screw you for saying I'm having a "Millennial moment."

MAN WITH THE VAN. But you are a Millennial.

PENNY. I'm not my generation, ok? My problems are specific to me. And even if I am my generation then answer me this: why is it that everyone else gets to go on this journey, every other generation gets to go out and find themselves, but when I do it you call it self-absorption and label me a Millennial brat. You Baby Boomers are so hypocritical.

MAN WITH THE VAN. I'm a Gen-Xer.

PENNY. Whatever. I just want my turn at this. On my own. Without everyone hovering over me trying to fix me.

MAN WITH THE VAN. Ok so the answer is what? Biking to god knows where 'til you're all tuckered out? At some point you'll still have to turn around and face up to the group.

PENNY. Not if I keep on biking.

MAN WITH THE VAN. Ah. So this isn't a stroll?

PENNY. It's a distance relationship. You guys are holding me back.

MAN WITH THE VAN. Little Penny. Take it from a grizzled Gen-Xer who's been down that road. You wanna burn all your bridges and cut yourself off from the world? Yeah man, that's the Gen-X anthem! Hell, I've even done it myself.

PENNY. I bet you have, because you got your turn.

MAN WITH THE VAN. Yeah, fine, guilty. I confess I was not always the grounded, well-put-together Adonis you see before you today. Which is why I can say with authority that what you're looking for, it ain't out there. You think being a lone wolf gives you power? No, it just means you're a coward. You think you're gonna find yourself out there? Naw kid. The truth is you already know who you are, and you just don't like it.

PENNY. But. But I'm the lady Tom Sawyer...

MAN WITH THE VAN. You're a smart kid but all this deflection won't hide the fact that you can't run away from yourself.

PENNY. I'm not running away, I'm running to.

MAN WITH THE VAN. Maybe maybe not, but your self discovery process does not entitle you to renounce your obligations to others. That's something that me and all the Gen-Xers and all the Baby Boomers and hippie dippie Thoreau types forgot. So don't just repeat our mistakes Penny. Come with me. Come make amends with your people.

PENNY. They're not my people. Not anymore.

MAN WITH THE VAN. Sure, you may feel that way *now* but…

PENNY. Look, Man, just stop. I have to go down this road. On my own. Even if there's *nothing down there* I have to go see for myself.

MAN WITH THE VAN. If you keep going like this I'm not gonna follow.

PENNY. Good. Then I'll see you at the Pacific Ocean.

(*PENNY gets on her bike and takes off. The* **MAN WITH THE VAN** *fades away and Lucinda Williams'* Jackson *starts playing.* **PENNY** *is biking along at an easy clip. She picks up the speed. The wind's at her back. She's smiling. The music is playing. She starts to push herself— really builds it up to a genuine workout. Adrenaline and endorphins. Biking. Biking. Just a girl and the night and the bike. Then, the ominous glare of headlights. Then the sound of a truck collision as the lights become blinding. Blackout.*)

22. Epilogue

PENNY. What's up you fuckers I'm dead. Do I have any regrets? Yes. Would I do it again? No.

The truck driver phoned in the accident just after he *awoke from the wheel.* That was thoughtful. He realized he'd turned his 53 foot trailer into a 44,000 pound penny-crushing machine. You remember those penny-crushing machines they have at museums where you put in 51 cents and out comes a flattened penny shaped like a scenic vista? That's pretty much the deal with me.

After the usual freakouts, the group pressed on and found the Pacific. They dipped their raw, weary feet in the waves and mumbled platitudes like, "Penny really would've liked this." And I'm like - yes. Yes, I would've liked this. I would've liked this a great deal more than being *smeared out like toothpaste* on the Arizona highway. And I felt these waves of regret at being a fuckup. And I felt these waves of regret at all the time I spent looking outwards, all that deflection when I should have just loved and lived. And I could have loved. Anyone. And I could have lived. Anywhere. Anywhere down that 4,000 mile expanse. There were 4,000 Pennies all down that route and yet I had to go and pick that one.

(The cast stands in a line down at the lip of the stage.)

They stood there, their feet in the sand, feeling the waves that I'd never feel, watching a sunset I'd never see. And they smiled and nodded like they knew me. And I thought, how could they know me? I still don't know me.

(The clicking sound of bicycle wheels. Ding ding! Lights out.)

End of Play

www.ingramcontent.com/pod-product-compliance
Lightning Source LLC
Chambersburg PA
CBHW070357120726
47909CB00008B/2891